The Terror Experience

By David G Evans

Table of Contents

Chapter 1 8

Chapter 2 19

Chapter 3 31

Chapter 4 42

Chapter 5 53

Chapter 6 65

Chapter 7 75

There was a facility that was one hundred feet down in the Pacific Ocean. The facility is called the great white shark, where great sharks are studied.

Clare has been studying how the great white shark lives in its natural habitat and its feeding habits. She's thirty years old and has a degree in biology.

She lives with her mom, Sara. Her mom is sickly and is on a special diet. She can have no salt in her diet and can't eat too much at one time. But she has a good dietician that's always looking out for her.

Sara is fifty years old and is always exercising, each morning she has a bagel and a scrambled egg.

She's not a picky eater and she likes to eat donuts but knows that they aren't good for her. Clare has worked at aquatic world and would love to play with the dolphins.

After just two years of working there she was feeling like she wasn't appreciated and the other trainers kept on saying that she wasn't doing her job.

They would pick apart everything that she would do on a daily basis. She knew all the dolphin's names and would give the dolphins rewards when they would do there tricks.

However, one of the dolphins had an attitude toward the other trainers and would slam into them pining them against the concrete wall.

This particular dolphins name was Ben and he was a bottle nosed dolphin. But he would never give Clare a problem, he was so loyal to her all of the time. When she quit working at aquatic world, she missed Ben the dolphin.

Shortly after she left aquatic world, Ben got sick and within two years passed away. It was a great loss for aquatic world and he'll always be remembered.

Clare loved to swim and was in two different swimming competitions where she won first place two times in a row. Her mom was so proud of her, that she mentioned to Clare that she should try out for the Olympics.

But with her busy schedule she didn't have the time for that. Clare currently doesn't have a boyfriend; she prefers to live alone. Clare was a star athlete while she was in high school.

She didn't like high school because some of the other girls would say that she was too perfect and shouldn't try so hard. But she would just ignore them and go on with her life.

Clare has always been interested in studying the ocean and the many species of fish that live in the ocean. Clare likes to go to the local beach and swim in the cool ocean water of the Pacific Ocean.

When she swims in the Pacific Ocean she puts on a wet suit so that the water temperature won't affect her.

When she swims she likes to pull her long hair back and slowly swim along. She likes to collect seashells from every beach that she visits; she has almost every size of seashell imaginable.

One day she was reading through her emails, and an ad popped up on the screen of her laptop. The ad said apply now to work at the great white facility.

In small print below the ad, it said work here at your own risk and don't worry the sharks don't bite too hard. She thought what am I getting myself into.

Clare took a moment and read on, the ad said that you're going to risk your life working here. She found a phone number on the ad and quickly took out her smart phone and dialed the number, it was a seven one seven number.

"She dialed it and it rang four times and someone picked and asked are you calling for a job?"

"Yes," I'm calling to get information on the job and what skills I might need for the job.

The gentleman she was talking to had a low voice and every so often he would pause in the middle of a sentence.

Chapter 1

He said my name is Owen, and I'm the owner of the company. It's nice to meet you Sir, don't call me Sir, I prefer to be called by my first name thanks.

"What's your name young lady?"

"My name is Clare, it's nice to meet you Clare. Alright divulge more about yourself?"

I have worked at aquatic world for two years training dolphins and I have a bachelor's degree in biology. That's great to hear and you know what I think you might be perfect for the job.

"What would I be doing at the facility?"

"First things first young lady, don't you want me to tell you about the facility itself?"

"Yes," I would like to know about it.

The facility itself is made up of three different sub floors. The bottom floor is fifty feet from the bottom of the Pacific Ocean, and the next floor is just thirty feet below the surface and the floor after that is eighty-five feet deep.

There are no elevators in the building, however there are plenty of reinforced windows that can withstand tons of pressure.

"When should I come in and meet with you?"

"Hold on you're getting ahead of yourself, each day I'll expect you to come in at nine o clock."

"Is that alright with you?"

"That's fine and I'm a morning person."

"What exactly do you do with the great white sharks?"

We have four great whites in captivity and were doing different experiments on them.

"Like what's done?"

"We're trying to see if we can make them more docile."

"How often have your workers been attacked?"

"Every so often, just last week one of the workers was killed and eaten by one of our sharks."

That's just horrible you should be ashamed of yourself for letting that happen. It was an accident, still that was someone else's life, I understand.

"Can you at least explain to me how it all happened?"

"No," I wasn't there over searing it. I was in my office and I got a call on my cell phone.

I have an assistant that's supposed to work with the biologists but doesn't always do what he's told and sometimes he has an attitude with me.

"Why don't you fire him then?"

"No," he has been working here for four years and I don't want to just get rid of him that fast.

"What else does your team do with the Sharks?"

There's one deep pool where the great white swims and the main objective is to find the cells that make the white sharks aggressive and eradicate the cells and see if the sharks can become as docile as a bottled nosed dolphin.

"Have you ever been successful at finding the cell?"

"No," and this is a government run program and we have funds coming in each day, so far we have collected upwards of just over fifty million dollars. That's a lot of cash, it sure is.

"Does the job sound interesting so far?"

"Yes," it does, I'm very interested in helping your team to find that certain cell.

I'm glad that I saw your ad on my computer.

"How about we meet tomorrow at the dock, and I'll take you for a trip around our facility?"

"What time would you like me there?"

"How about nine o clock?"

"That'll be okay and I can hear the excitement in your voice."

"Do you know what the starting rate will be for me?"

We'll discuss that once you're hired, alright that sounds good to me. The dock where Owen wanted to meet Clare was thirty minutes away from her apartment.

Clare got up and got dressed and walked into the kitchen area and picked up a new unopened box of lucky charm cereal.

She looked down at her silver wristwatch and it showed that it was six fifty-five. She thought to herself well I now have plenty of time to meet Owen.

She filled up her small cereal bowl with the cereal and poured low fat milk over the cereal. She was so excited that she didn't waste time finishing up her cereal.

She walked over to the sink and turned on the water and washed out the bowl. She went back into her room after finishing her breakfast and opened up her closet.

In the bottom of the closet was a nice leather briefcase. This is where she keeps all of her records and certificates from her years at college.

She liked to keep all the records nice and neat. She went over to her desk and her laptop was sitting there, she quickly picked it up along with her nice leather briefcase.

She opened the front door and quickly walked outside, she placed her laptop and briefcase on the passenger seat.

Her car was a bright yellow 2021 sports car. She has had this car for less than a month, she bought it from the nearby sports car dealership. Her mom had given her the money to buy the car.

She's lucky that her mom loves her that much. Today was such a good day for her, the sun was shining and it was getting close to eighty degrees, the sky was blue and there were a few white clouds in the sky. Clare arrived a few minutes early at the dock, she got out of her car and tightly held onto her briefcase and laptop.

She slowly walked over to the end of dock and sat down. There was no cool breeze blowing and the sun was hot. Her long blond hair kept on going in her face, she carefully sat down the laptop and briefcase right next to her.

She pulled out a rubber band from her pocket and used it to tie her hair up. The morning seemed to be moving along at a snail's pace.

Clare was so excited to begin working for Owen. A pelican flew past the dock; its mouth was full of small fish. She saw a sea gull land on the end post of the dock, it must have had a nest somewhere nearby.

Suddenly a little motorboat was moving along slowly towards the dock. It was Owen, he was wearing a gray suit and red tie.

He was wearing a baseball cap and had a big smile on his face, he looked over at her and the sun caused him to sneeze. Clare said god bless you and he said thanks.

"Are you ready to board the boat?"

"Yes," I'm ready to board.

"Would you like me to carry your laptop and briefcase for you?"

"Yes," I please, I would really appreciate that.

Chapter 2

Owen carefully took her stuff and placed it in the boat next to him.

"How come were in a small motorboat?"

"What were you looking for an elaborate ship?"

"No," but I wasn't expecting to be in a small motorboat.

"Let's move on, how many employees do you have currently working for you?"

I have six employees and they're hard workers except for the one guy that I was telling you about earlier.

Now all of my workers wear an identification badge and they also have two keys.

"What are the two keys for?"

"The one key is for the security doors and the other for your locker and your own room."

"You mean that I'll have my own room, yes. That's just great, it makes me even more excited."

Now it's time for us to get out of the boat and we're now on the top floor of the facility. Let me hand you your briefcase and laptop. Thank you and let me open the main door and let's begin walking down the two flights of steps.

You definitely get your exercise working at this place. I always need exercise; I don't have a really good diet.

I'm a junk food junkie and my favorite treat is donuts. Enough about me, let me tell you more about the sharks.

"Did you name any of these sharks?"

"Yes."

"What did you name it?"

"Dart."

"Why do you call him dart?"

"Because when he was a baby, he would dart around the training pool."

"Are you going to show me the training pool today?"

"I most definitely will, and I'll introduce you to my workers and my assistant."

Once were at the bottom of the second flight of stairs we'll be in the middle of the facility. This area is the most secure area of the whole facility. If the facility were to flood this is where you would go and swim to the surface.

"Suddenly Owen began to cough, what's the matter?"

"I'm just getting over a bad cold."

You didn't have that before; I didn't think it would be a big deal to you.

"Is it?"

"No," it's not.

I'm going to introduce you to my assistant Evan. Owen opened a heavy pressure sealed door and inside there was a rather tall figure. He was staring over at the small window.

"How are you doing today?"

"I'm doing good, just going through the same routine."

"How's my team doing?"

"They're all good and accounted for."

"They're getting ready to do some research, research on what?"

"They're currently researching how the sharks brain functions."

Tell them that I have someone that I want them to meet, I'll get on the radio and inform them.

"How soon do you think we all could meet?"

"I would say in fifteen minutes. Alright that sounds good."

I'll be right back, just wait here. Clare kept on looking around the room, on the far wall there was a map of the world and a depth map of the Pacific Ocean.

On the wall off to the left of her was a picture of someone surfing. She didn't recognize who it was in the picture.

In the corner of the room was a big brown desk and the top of the desk had a stack of papers on it.

There was a gold key on top of all the papers and there was a rolled-up poster that was on the edge of the desk. She took a closer look and saw a paper that said top secret on it.

She wondered what else it said, but was too afraid to read more. She didn't want to get into trouble.

"What do you think of the place so far?"

"I like it, but I still have a lot of unanswered questions."

"Why don't you ask me now all of your questions?"

"I will but I was going to wait, no there's no need to wait."

I'd like to know what you do for security.

"Do you have any spear guns or anything like that to protect yourselves against the sharks?"

"Yes," we have the top-of-the-line spear guns and we have pistols and assault rifles in the vault.

"Where's the vault located?"

"It's located right beneath this floor."

To make you feel better, I'll show you our weapons room.

We have to wait for my team to come up here and meet with you and me.

"Have you ever used the weapons on the sharks?"

"Yes," we have, we have five great whites and an Edestus shark and one of the great whites went rogue and began to not respond to anything that we were doing to help it.

"What was the name of that shark?"

"We don't take the time to name all of the sharks because it doesn't matter. The shark was known as the test shark. We named him that because he was the first shark that we began to experiment on."

"Was he the shark that ate one of your team members?"

"Yes," and it was a terrible incident that I don't like to think about.

I felt so bad for the guy's family. We have one other female worker, but the rest of the crew are guys. Each of the workers are given a pump action shotgun once they're hired.

"You mean I'll get one too?"

"Yes," you will.

It's just a simple pump shotgun that's all. I prefer to shoot the five hundred pistol; I like the knock down power that it has.

"Who was the person who killed this rogue shark?"

"I did, the Pentagon called here and talked to me over the radio system and they said that I should destroy the monster shark before it had a chance to hurt others."

"What kind of weapon did you use to shoot the shark with?"

"I used my special assault rifle; I shot the shark in the head and I used an armor piercing round. I wanted to ensure that he was dead, I took no chances."

I'm sorry to hear that, I'm the kind of guy who doesn't waste time worrying about anything.

That's good to hear, the door opened and five guys and another woman walked in. They all had smiles on their faces, and all were wearing white lab coats and scrub pants.

I want to introduce you to Shannon; she answers the phones and keeps the records kept together. Next up is Jack, he's in charge of security around here. Michael is in charge of our machinery.

Chapter 3

The second to last is Franky, he's the chief and last is Dewey, he's the medic. All the guys came over and Clare shook their hands and smiled and said it's nice to meet all of you. Everyone seemed like they were in a rush and they filed out one by one out of the office.

The room was getting hot and the air wasn't circulating very well. Clare was beginning to get hot and could feel the sweat pouring down her forehead.

She had nothing to wipe her forehead off with. I'm going to take you down to the bottom floor of the facility and show you the training pool. Before you show me that, I have a question for you about one of the sharks.

"What's an Edestus shark?"

"It's a type of extinct shark that existed during the Late Carboniferous Period about 300 million years ago."

How did you bring it back to life?"

"I didn't bring it back to life, a good friend of mine gave it to me who is a geneticist."

"Are there going to be any sharks in the training pool?"

"Yes," the one female great white shark will be in the training pool.

Now let's continue down two flights of steps and then we'll be on the bottom floor. Ten minutes later they were on the bottom floor of the facility.

Owen opened a heavy pressurized door and they walked onto the platform of the training pool. The great white shark was swimming around in circles; this shark was displaying strange behavior.

"Clare asked Owen why's this shark swimming around in a circle?"

"Honestly I don't know why."

"It could be from the experiments that we have done on the shark."

Why don't you take a walk around don't worry it's safe, I know it's safe but I can see everything that I want to see just from standing here. Clare pointed to a large machine that had three switches on it and asked what it was used for.

This machine costs a million dollars and makes low pitched noises that only the shark can hear. This white shark is acting so calm now.

"Why did it stop circling around?"

"I don't have an answer for you, I'm sorry. You don't have to be sorry; you can't know everything."

"Would you mind if I bent down and tried to pet the shark on its head?" asked Clare.

"I wouldn't try that."

"Why not?"

"The shark seems calm enough and seems to be happy in its environment. Alright but don't slip and fall in, I don't want to lose you to the shark."

Clare slowly bent down on one knee and reached down and petted the shark on the top of its head, suddenly it tried to rise up out of the water.

It splashed its tail and water went all over Clare; the water felt so cold and was refreshing. She stood up and walked away from the edge of the training pool.

"What happened?"

"The shark let me pet her on top of her head. That's great to hear, and she didn't try to bite you."

She seemed to stay calm the whole time that I was petting her.

"Were you terrified of the shark?"

"Yes," answered Clare.

My team would never do what you just did, it's just not safe.

"Are you afraid of these sharks?"

"No," but I don't want to be there friend, I just work with the sharks.

"Would you kill another shark if you had to?"

"Yes," I would.

"How are your parents doing?"

"My mom died just four years ago from a shark attack."

My dad is getting older and more forgetful as time goes on.

"Does he remember you?"

"Yes," he does, but he sometimes thinks that I'm his uncle but other than that he's doing good.

"What do you think of the training pool?"

"I think that I'm ready to work here tomorrow."

"Would you like my cell phone number or my email address?"

"I just need your email."

"Do you have something that I can write my email address on?"

"Sure, I do here's a pen and paper thanks."

"Are you done showing me around?"

"No," not yet I want to show you the weapons vault yet.

Come with me and I'll show you, we have to go down three big steps then we'll be at the vault.

"Does the vault have a pressure sealed door?"

"Yes," it does

"Has this facility ever been flooded before?"

"No," and's there an alarm that'll sound if this place does begin to flood.

Owen opened the pressurized door and they both walked into the room. There were two tables that were painted red in the middle of the room.

There were guns stacked up and there was a row of shotguns, that were leaning up against the wall and there were spear guns right next to them. In the back corner of the room, were extra scuba masks and wet suits.

There was a small table to the far side of the room, on the table were flares and three flare guns. I've seen enough of this room, let's go, then you can leave.

Clare could hear someone screaming over the radio that was in Owens shirt pocket.

"What's that screaming?"

"It's an emergency, why don't you stay here in the weapons room and I'll be right back."

"What do you think happened?"

"I don't know but I got to go."

I hope everything will be alright, and Owen never answered her back. Clare pulled up a chair and sat down.

She was thinking in her mind, I hope the situation isn't too dire and I hope that Owen comes back soon.

The hallway was silent and Clare didn't hear anything. She began to lean over in the chair and her gold cross necklace fell off of her neck and landed on the floor in front of her. She leaned over and picked it up and placed the necklace in her right-side pocket.

Clare was beginning to feel bored and stood up and wandered down the hallway. At the end of the hall was a window, she looked out the window and saw a great white shark swimming a few yards away from the window.

This great white shark looked like it was thirty-five feet long. It had a scar near its left eye, it turned and to its other side and had no right eye but instead of an eye it had a false eye that was red and looked like it was a laser.

Chapter 4

It had large teeth that looked larger than a regular great white's teeth. Now it was swimming directly towards the window.

It seemed to be going rogue and wanted to bust through the window. Clare was terrified of this shark and tried to walk backwards.

She tripped and the shark continued to come closer and closer, it shook her up so badly that she began to scream in pure terror.

The shark hit the window so hard that it had cracks in it but no water came in. Clare made sure to stay back from that particular window. She walked back over to the vault room and sat back down in the chair.

She was shaking and thought to herself, I bet one of the sharks ate another one of the team members.

Owen came walking down the hallway and saw that Clare was sitting down on a chair with her head down.

"Are you alright?"

"Yes," I'm alright.

"What happened?"

I just went over to the window at the end of the hallway and looked out and saw a huge great white shark. It looked like it was a thirty-five-footer. That's one of the great white sharks that we have here and he's the most dangerous of all the white sharks.

"How come, he's missing his right eye?"

"It was part of an experiment that went wrong."

"Is everything alright?"

"Yes," one of my team members got their leg ripped off by the shark that you just petted on the head.

"How did they get bitten?"

"They slipped and fell into the training pool, when they tried to get back out of the pool the shark caught him by his leg and tore his left leg off but didn't eat it."

My team pulled him out, and he's being treated for his wounds. Everything is good at the moment; I'm going to get going then and I'll see you tomorrow. Owen called a meeting with all of his employees, in the vault room. His employees were excited to see what he was going to say to them.

All of you have met our new recruit Clare, but I'm still not sure if I fully trust her to work here. From the time I spent with her she was very nosy about what we do around here.

I told her everything that she wanted to know, just to keep her quiet. I'm sure that everyone here remembers the one employee that was killed by the shark and eaten by it. Then something caused the shark to regurgitate the body, and that's when I did something I should have never done, and that was trying to play God.

None of you need to stay silent, just speak up and tell me what you're thinking.

"Michael raised his arm; can you tell me again how you rejuvenated that dead guy?"

"I took the mosquito DNA that I stole from a secret lab and mixed it with shark DNA."

An hour after that the dead man woke up, and when his body began to transform into something unrecognizable I got out of that room. I haven't opened the window on the door to look in on the thing yet today.

"What do you call it?"

"You remember what I call it."

Go ahead and say it Michael don't be afraid; it's called the shark mosquito man. Shannon brought up her hand, don't you think that the shark mosquito man is suffering the way he's living.

No, he's not suffering. I give him two pieces of steak twice a day, and a bowl full of electrolyte water, so that he doesn't get dehydrated.

The bowl is usually empty after three hours goes by, that shows me that he's intelligent enough to take a drink.

"Why don't you go in the room and sit with him for a while?"

"No," because I don't know how he'll act.

He could be a nice monster you never know; believe me I watched him eat the piece of meat and he eats it like a rabid animal would. Next time I feed him, I'm going to have you stand by the door to watch what he does through the window.

You said that in an offlay mean manner, it's because I'm tired of that thing. I highly doubt that you are, you're probably thinking about figuring out a way to study that thing.

"Each time you looked at that thing did it have wings?"

"Yes," it had wings, and had a weird looking face.

Its face was crossed between a mosquito and a shark. Dewey spoke out loud, I've gone past the door several times and looked at that thing and it just scared me to death.

"You do realize that thing is going to find a way out of here?"

"Yes," I do realize that.

That'll put us all in harm's way, but you don't seem to care. It's like you have some kind of relationship with that thing, just kill the thing and throw it in with the sharks.

No, I'm not ready to do that yet, I'd like to see how much longer it'll live for. That's just crazy, you're getting way out of line.

"Have you tried to talk to the thing?"

"No," and it probably wouldn't understand our language anyway.

I think it might understand because it used to be a human, that has nothing to do with it. I doubt that it even remembers being a human anymore.

"Do you think it would drink blood?"

"Yes," because it's part mosquito and that's what they do.

It's a male mosquito and the female mosquitoes are the ones that bite. You should try taking a lab mouse and putting it in that room with the thing, then watch what happens.

I'm sure it'll chase after it and once it gets it, it'll drain it of its blood then eat it. You keep acting like you know all of its behavior, and you don't know. Maybe it'll be nice and friendly to it, and even become his friend.

Then who knows maybe the thing and the mouse will find a way to communicate with one another, I'm sure that the next thing that you'll do, is say there would be no way it could happen.

You're right I should stop putting this thing down. We can't allow Clare to see the thing, or even go in room 10 where it resides. If she asks about room ten just tell her that's off limits, and that's where we keep our classified documents.

"What if she asks again about it when you're not here?"

"Tell her if she goes in that room she'll be arrested for trespassing."

If you do break down and tell her about the room then you're going to be fired. But I'll be leaving in four days, to visit a new biochemical lab in Arkansas.

Chapter 5

Shannon whispered in Frankie's ear; I can't wait to get out of here. Maybe if we ask him more difficult questions, he'll stop the meeting.

"Are you ever going to release dart into the wild?"

"Yes."

I thought for sure you would have said no, but I'm happily surprised.

"Is there anything about dart that you've kept a secret?"

"Yes."

While I was working with him a few weeks ago, I saw a rash on his back. When I touched the rash, it felt like hard scales. Then I mixed up some shark rash salve and I put on gloves and took some of the salve and put it on my gloves then spread it over the rash.

"How much of an area did the rash cover?"

"Four inches."

"How long did it take the rash to go away?"

"Two days."

That's the reason why he was in shark sick bay. That was the first time ever I had to put him in shark sick bay. The Edestus shark has been calmer than normal these days.

"What can you contribute that to?"

"I'm not sure."

That shark tried to nip me the other day, I don't think it likes me. You used to tell us how important it was for this shark to get its vitamins, every day. Now you tell us that it doesn't need its vitamins.

"What caused you to change your mind?"

"An article that I read about sharks. I haven't read much about sharks anymore, and I know that I should be."

"Do you remember when we showed you the tooth that had fallen out of this sharks mouth?"

"Yes," I remember it very well.

Somehow you knew exactly what it was deficient in and gave it a calcium supplement. We have so much medicine and supplements for the sharks around here that we could open our own pharmacy.

We're all just glad that you and your assistant know what medicines treat what illnesses in the sharks. Jack was getting tired of sitting and got up and began walking around the room.

While Owen was talking to everyone, jack opened the door and walked out of the room. Then he went over to the window and looked out, a small shark swam past the window.

A few minutes later, he saw a huge two-headed hammerhead shark. Suddenly it lunched forward and slammed into the side of the building, Jack ran down the hall and entered the conference room. He waited until Owen was done speaking, then he spoke.

In a frantic voice he said the two headed hammerhead is back. Owen quickly exited the room and went over to the window with Jack.

As they were watching they saw a second huge hammerhead swim by, someone is going to have to get in the submersible to drive these sharks away from here.

It's been a year and a half since these hammer heads were here last, and they caused a lot of damage to this place.

"Do you know if the mosquito shark man can swim?"

"No," I don't.

But we should figure out a way to test it, but right now we have a shark problem.

"How long has it been since you have been in a submersible?"

"A month ago."

Since you have your doubts about me controlling the submersible, then have Evan go out in the submersible.

Then Evan came walking down the hall, excuse me Evan but I have to talk to you about something. Jack rolled his eyes and sat down in the chair by the window.

"Would you be comfortable with controlling the submersible and driving these huge sharks out of here?"

"Yes," I'm okay with it.

I'll get in the submersible as soon as I can, you won't have to worry about those sharks for much longer. Evan quickly made his way down the hall and entered his office. He accidentally brushed up against his desk knocking over a few important papers.

After picking up the papers he let out a yawn, then opened the cabinet behind him and took out an energy drink. He opened it and took a sip of it and put it down on his desk.

A few minutes later he got up and made his way down to the submersible bay. Meanwhile Owen and Jack were on their way to check on the mosquito shark man, the other employees left the conference room.

It was awfully rude of Owen not to tell us that the meeting was over, he's acting like a different man these days.

As Owen and Jack were walking down the hall they heard a buzzing sound coming from above them.

"What do you think is making that buzzing sound up there?"

"A bunch of bugs."

I just can't think of an explanation to why those bugs would be up there. The ceiling tile above them began to shake, then it came down.

Suddenly a swarm of mosquitoes came flying down after them, they quickly ran to the storage room and slammed the door behind them.

"Now what are we going to do?"

"We're just going to quietly discuss what we're going to do about the mosquitoes."

Okay but they may be after your other employees, I realize that but we can't protect them right now.

The chemicals in this spray bottle should be able to kill the mosquitoes, you can carry the spray bottle and I'll carry the mop.

When they opened the door there were no signs of the mosquitoes, I doubt that anyone has checked on dart for a while.

They made their way down the hall, until they came to the pool area. I'm sure that he's hungry by now, Owen set down his spray bottle on the table in front of him and Jack dropped the mop on the floor. We looked so silly back there walking around with cleaning supplies and a mop.

"Where do you think those mosquitoes got to?"

"I think that they joined the mosquito shark man."

Owen opened up the meat container, and took out a piece of steak, then he walked down the side of the pool until he came to where the shark was. The moment that the shark sensed that he was there it brought up its head and snapped its jaws at him.

He stepped back and lost his balance and fell into another one of the shark pools. His body immediately tensed up, and the piece of steak fell to the bottom of the pool.

The shark smelled blood and came charging towards him, he quickly got up out of the water, and the shark narrowly missed grabbing his foot.

"I saw what just happened are you alright?"

"Yes," but my heart feels like it's like it's going to beat out of my chest.

Chapter 6

I'll probably have nightmares for a week after seeing that shark under the water. This is the shark that has a tooth growing problem, I tried repeatedly to cure it.

Perhaps you should try again while we're here, I'll try again tomorrow to cure it. In another half an hour our workday is over, I'm awfully glad of that.

I'm going to go put the cleaning stuff away and I'll be back. Just don't go near those pools until I get back, don't you worry I won't I learned my lesson. He kept an eye on the sharks, watching what they were doing.

One of the sharks slammed its tail into the sides of the pool, and water splashed everywhere. A few minutes later Jack returned, I saw Shannon walking down the hallway.

She told me that the mosquitoes had come into her office and she sprayed them with hairspray and it killed them. She told me that she couldn't talk very long because she had to go use the restroom so bad.

Her hair was a mess and she was flustered, but other than that she was unharmed from the mosquitoes.

> "What caused this water to get all over the floor?"

> "The sharks caused that to happen."

I've never seen the sharks splash around like this so much, maybe they're angry about something. It's probably because they haven't moved for a while and they're moving their tails to keep them from tightening up.

Owen and Jack dried up the wet floor, using several towels. I think that we better head over to the submersible bay to check on Evan. I'm just hoping that he wasn't in an accident out there with those huge sharks.

I'm sure that he's just fine and will be returning soon. They exited the room and walked a short ways down the hallway until they came to room ten.

A few minutes later Evan came walking down the hall, we're so glad to see you. Everything went very well for me, I set off a depth charge that killed one of the hammerhead sharks. If either one of you need anything else, I'll be in my office and he walked away.

"How come the explosion didn't shake this place?"

"Because I set it off as far away from here as I could."

Meanwhile back at Clare's place, she was comfortably nestled into her couch curled up under her blanket reading her favorite book and had her phone on the small table next to the couch.

Her phone began ringing, and her phone showed that it was an unknown caller. She put her book down and grabbed her phone and answered it. Hello, this is Clare, I have something very important to tell you.

"What's your name?"

"My name is Jen."

"Have you applied at a new place to work?"

"Yes," I have.

"What's the place called?"

"The great white facility."

From what I hear that's a very dangerous place with many secrets, some really bad things have happened there. But they told me just about everything, no, they didn't. The sharks that dwell in that facility are extremely aggressive, if you accidentally fall into one of those shark pools, you'd be eaten on the spot. But I was able to pet one of the sharks, that's quite impressive.

"How many secrets are there in that place?"

"Four secrets."

I can't tell you the main secret of that place, what a letdown that is. I'll give you one million dollars if you destroy that facility and murder Owen. Believe me it wouldn't be hard to destroy that facility and find and murder Owen.

"How do you know him?"

"I used to date him."

"Do you have a gun that you can take with you tomorrow?"

"Yes," I do.

After you kill him and destroy the facility I'll pay you the money the next day. I'm not affiliated with the police or anyone like that.

Killing another person isn't that bad, I can't believe that you just said that. I killed two people, but I'll never get caught.

You don't know that though, oh I do. When you have done your deeds meet me at the delta gas station, on crude street at ten am.

I have to go bye now and she hung up the phone. This conversation had left Clare puzzled, and the whole night she was tossing and turning in bed.

Eventually at two am she quit tossing and turning and slept until six am, when she woke up. Then she went to take a quick shower, she dried herself off and she quickly put on her clothes.

She went into the kitchen and poured herself some cereal, that she took out of one of the cabinets.

She walked over to the refrigerator and opened it up and took out milk, that she poured over her cereal. Then grabbed a spoon from the utensil drawer and started eating the cereal.

After she was done eating she took her bowl and washed it out in the sink. She unplugged her smart phone that was plugged into the kitchen receptacle.

She was glad to see that the phone showed one-hundred percent charge, after that she headed into the room where she had her gun safe, she opened the safe and took out her pistol then closed the safe backup.

She grabbed her purse and placed the gun in the purse and placed her phone in her pocket and exited her house. But today she didn't take her laptop or briefcase with her.

An hour later she reached the dock, but Owen wasn't there and she took the small boat over to the entrance of the facility and entered the place.

She went down two hallways before coming to Owen's office. His office door was closed so she knocked on it, and he opened the door. Hello Clare, it's good to see you today, likewise.

"What do you have for me to do today?"

"Just some research."

Chapter 7

When he went to close his office door, she brought her gun out and pointed the gun at him and he brought his arms up surrendering to her.

"What's this all about now?"

"I was told by one of your exes, that If I killed you and destroyed this place she would give me one million dollars.

Tell me the biggest secret of this place or I'm going to hit you with my gun. The biggest secret is that I brought a dead man back to life and he turned into a creature. Don't you dare try to wrestle this gun out of my hands.

"Where are your other employees?"

"They're working right now."

"Are you going to make me announce to them that you have me held up in my office?"

"No."

"Can you take me to where the creature is?"

"Yes," I will.

She had her gun pointed to his head as they made their way down the hallway to room ten. Now I want you to open the door and go in there, he hesitated for a moment and she hit him with her gun in the side of the face.

After he entered the room, she entered the room with him and the mosquito shark man was standing in the back of the room.

That's the ugliest thing I've seen in a long time. I'm surprised that it hasn't attacked one of us by now. I should just shoot that thing dead right now, nobody else will hear the gun go off because it has a silencer.

Suddenly the creature moved closer to them. Clair backed up from Owen, and when she did the mosquito shark man grabbed him by the arm and dragged him to the back of the room and tore his head off.

She looked over and saw a few oxygen tanks, then she shot the mosquito shark man several times and he collapsed.

She took out her lighter and set a piece of paper on fire and threw it on the floor and quickly ran out of the room.

She was surprised that she hadn't ran into anyone in the hallway yet, she walked on until she came to the main entrance then exited the place.

She fired up the small boat and took off back to the dock, then got in her car and took off out of there.

Everyone in the facility we're concentrating on what they were doing, not knowing what was about to happen to them.

An oxygen tank went up through the ceiling and exploded where their main inventory of ninety-six oxygen tanks were kept along with other highly flammable items.

The explosion was so intense that it caused an earthquake, sadly no one lived through the explosion, not even the fearsome sharks.

Pieces of the building quickly plummeted to the bottom of the Pacific Ocean, there were no remains of the people or the sharks to be found.

The next day Clare drove to the Delta gas station at ten am and met with Jen, who said hello to her and gave her a million dollars in cash, then they parted ways.

After two days of no communication, between the facility and the pentagon, a team of armed soldiers were sent to the dock to see what was going on there.

After they arrived there, they didn't even see the facility. They mentioned this to their superior and he had them start an investigation.

The End

Printed in Great Britain
by Amazon